P9-CKQ-104

# Three Clever Mice

Folktales retold
and adapted by

### Gerda Mantinband

Illustrated by

### Martine Gourbault

Greenwillow Books
New York

Library of Congress Cataloging-in-Publication Data
Mantinband, Gerda.
Three clever mice / [retold and adapted] by
Gerda Mantinband ; pictures by Martine Gourbault.
p.   cm.
Summary: Three folktales featuring mouse
characters, from Turkey, Japan, and Nepal.
ISBN 0-688-11369-9.  ISBN 0-688-11370-2  (lib. bdg.)
1. Tales.   [1. Folklore. 2. Mice — Folklore.]
I. Gourbault, Martine, ill.   II. Title.
PZ8.1.M2987Th    1993
398.24′5293233 — dc20
[E]    91-48171    CIP    AC

FOR PEGGY

# CONTENTS

♦ ♦ ♦

# Will You Marry Me, Miss Mouse?

### ◆ A MOUSE TALE FROM TURKEY ◆

Once a little mouse lived all alone in a little house. In the mornings she did her chores and then sat at the piano to write the songs she sang while she tended her flower garden. In the afternoons she sat by her window and watched the world go by.

People passing her house often stopped and said, "How do you do, Miss Mouse?"

"Very well, thank you," she always answered.

But one day she suddenly thought, It's getting a bit

lonely singing by myself. It would be more fun to have someone to sing with me.

It was a sunny afternoon when a handsome rabbit stopped by her window.

"How do you do, Miss Mouse?" he said.

"Very well, thank you," the little mouse replied. "But it's getting a bit lonesome around here."

"Then marry me!" the rabbit said.

"I do like your nice long ears," said the mouse. "But can you sing?"

The rabbit wrinkled his nose. "Sing?" he said. "I never tried, but let me see." He opened his mouth, but not one note of music came out.

"No," said the mouse. "You can't sing, and I can't marry you." And the rabbit hopped sadly away.

Not long after that, a handsome peacock strutted down the street.

"How do you do, Miss Mouse?" he said.

"Very well, thank you," the mouse replied. "But it's getting a little lonesome around here."

"Then marry me!" said the peacock, and he spread his many-colored tail.

"I do like your beautiful feathers," said the mouse. "But can you sing?"

The peacock opened his mouth, and such a harsh, raucous sound came out of it that the little mouse had to clap both paws over her ears.

"That's not music!" she cried. "I can't marry you." And the peacock folded his tail and went away.

Another day a rooster stopped at the mouse's window.

"How do you do, Miss Mouse?" he said.

"Very well, thank you," the mouse replied. "But it's getting a little lonesome around here."

"Then marry me!" the rooster said.

"I do like your bright red comb," said the mouse. "But can you sing?"

The rooster opened his beak and sang such a lovely cock-a-doodle-doo that the mouse clapped her paws for joy and cried, "Oh! Oh! What beautiful music! Certainly I will marry you. Then we can sing duets together."

So the rooster wrapped his soft wings around the mouse. He lifted her from the window and carried her to the church, where they were married.

Now the rooster left the house early every morning to go about his crowing business, after which he went to the coffeehouse where he chatted with his friends.

The little mouse wrote a new song each day. Then she cooked dinner, and when the rooster came home, she filled their plates. They ate their food, sang a duet, and went to bed.

But one day the little mouse had stoked the fire too high. When she lifted the lid off the soup pot, the steam shot up and scalded her. She fell on the floor and didn't move.

That day the rooster came home and knocked on the door, but no one let him in. He knocked and knocked. There was no answer. Finally he went to the back door, and it was open. He entered the kitchen. There was his little mouse lying motionless on the floor.

"Little mouse, little mouse," he called, but she didn't stir.

So he stood over her and fanned her with his wings for three days and three nights. He never stopped fanning until, on the fourth morning, the little mouse gave a big sigh and opened her eyes. But when she sat up to talk to her rooster, he had fainted for joy!

She hurried to get some water and poured it over him, and he soon revived. Then she led him to the table, and at breakfast she told him how the soup had scalded her.

When they had finished eating, the rooster said, "Little mouse, let's forget about my crowing and your songs today. Let's just go to the coffeehouse and enjoy ourselves together." And that's what they did.

And after that, every day when the rooster finished his crowing business, he went straight home for dinner. They ate and washed the dishes, and then they both went to the coffeehouse and sang for their friends. Sometimes only the two of them sang, and sometimes their friends joined in.

Usually there was a chorus of "cluck, cluck, cluck" from a bunch of hens, a "quack, quack, quack" from a gaggle of geese, and "tsiu, tsiu, tsiu" from a flock of pigeons.

Pretty soon the musicians in the village wanted to join in, and the pig brought his fiddle, the goat his horn, and the donkey his trumpet. The concerts brought people from all over the countryside to listen to the music, and the rooster and the little mouse were the happiest couple in the village.

# The Sun, the Cloud, the Wind, and the Wall

◆ A MOUSE TALE FROM JAPAN ◆

A father and a mother mouse once had a daughter they thought beautiful beyond compare. When she grew up, she fell in love with a young mouse who lived nearby. But neither he nor any of the other mice who wanted to marry her were good enough, her parents decided.

"Only the most powerful one in all of Japan deserves such a lovely young mouse for his wife," they said. Finally they decided that the sun that shines over all the land was the suitable husband for their daughter.

The young mouse didn't want to marry the sun, but

14
◆

she was an obedient daughter, and so she went with her parents to find the sun.

When at last they reached the sun, the mouse father bowed low in greeting and said, "All-powerful sun, here

is our beautiful daughter, whom we wish to give in marriage to the mightiest being in all Japan."

"I am much honored," answered the sun. "But I am not the mightiest, as you seem to think. There is one more powerful than I."

"How can that be?" cried the mouse parents. "When the sun doesn't shine, the earth grows dark and cold. How could anyone be more powerful than that?"

"Indeed," said the sun, "I would like to shine all the time and give light and warmth to the world. But when the great cloud comes along and covers my rays, what can I do then?"

"How true!" the mice agreed, and they took their reluctant daughter and went to find the cloud.

"All-powerful cloud," they said when they reached him, "you who sends rain to make the rice grow, here is our beautiful daughter, whom we wish to give in marriage to the mightiest being in all Japan."

"You are most kind, and I am honored," said the cloud. "But there is one mightier than I. When the wind comes along, I have to go wherever he blows me."

"How true," the mice agreed. They bid the cloud good-bye, took their unwilling daughter, and went to find the wind.

"All-powerful wind," they said when they found him, "you who blow over the earth and ocean, behold our beautiful daughter, whom we wish to give in marriage to the mightiest being in all Japan."

"Alas!" said the wind. "You are mistaken. There is one mightier than I. When a strong wall stands in my way, I cannot blow it down."

"He is right," said the mice, and they took their weeping daughter and went to find the wall.

But the wall said, "No, no, I am not the mightiest.

There is a little mouse who lives nearby. When he makes holes in me, there is nothing I can do."

The mouse parents were dumbfounded. A mouse the mightiest being in all of Japan? Who would ever have thought it! Then they said, "Very well, he shall have our daughter."

The young mouse's whiskers trembled with joy. She would be allowed to marry her love! A mouse's wife was just what she wanted to be.

A splendid wedding was held at the foot of the wall. The sun shone on the couple, the cloud gave them shade when it grew too hot, the wind fanned them with gentle breezes, and they lived contentedly to a ripe old age.

# Mouse's Children

A little mouse was building her nest near the king's palace—a soft, warm nest, because she knew that soon she would give birth to a child. How surprised she was when, instead of a mouse, she bore a tiger cub!

The young tiger was playful and frisky and gave his mother much joy. But soon he was grown and said to the mouse, "Mother, I must go and live in the forest with the other tigers. But don't be sad. Whenever you need me, I will come back."

He pulled a handful of hairs from his shiny coat, saying, "Should you be in trouble, come to the edge of the forest, throw the hairs in the air, and call my name three times." Then the tiger left.

The mouse felt lonely without the tiger until, to her great joy, she found that she was going to have another child. When the time came, she gave birth not to a mouse, but to a peacock.

While the peacock was young, his mother feasted her eyes on his feathers, which shone in all the colors of the rainbow. But soon he, too, grew up and said, "Mother, it is time that I earned my own living like all the other birds in the forest. I must leave you. But don't be sad. Should you ever need me, I will come back."

He pulled three feathers from his wing and added, "When you want me, go to the edge of the forest and throw these feathers into the air. Then call my name three times, and I will come to you." Then the peacock left.

Now the mother mouse was alone again, and she thought, What is the use of having children when they leave you as soon as they are grown? If ever I have another child, I'll make sure to keep him home.

Imagine her joy when a third child was born—not a mouse, not a tiger or peacock, but a human boy!

When he grew older, his mother told him about his brothers and how they had left her to go and live in the forest.

"But you can't do that," she said. "You are a human boy, and you would perish in the wilderness. You must stay near the nest."

So the boy stayed near the nest and never wandered far away.

One day the town barber, who often cut the king's hair, noticed the boy and offered to give him a haircut. The boy agreed, and soon the barber was snipping away. But the boy's hair, as it fell to the ground, turned into diamonds, pearls, and rubies! The boy was as surprised as the barber. The barber dropped his scissors, let them lie where they fell, and ran to see the king.

"Your Majesty, Your Majesty!" he shouted, without even taking time to be announced. "There's a boy outside who grows precious jewels on his head!"

The king was a wealthy man, but he was also greedy and deceitful. He ordered the boy to be brought before him and said, "I have heard that you have been loitering near the palace and that your mother has built a nest nearby without permission. As punishment I will have your mother killed and make you my slave—unless you do as I ask.

"You must bring me four tigers, the biggest and strongest you can find, to guard the gates of the palace. If you succeed, you can save your mother and yourself, and I will give you my daughter for your wife and half my kingdom as well."

The boy ran home in tears and told his mother what the king had said.

"Don't be afraid," the mouse said. "Your brother the tiger will help you." She gave the boy the handful of tiger's hairs and told him to go to the edge of the forest, throw the hairs into the air, and call his brother three times.

The boy walked and walked until he came to the forest's edge. There he did as his mother had told him.

Soon a low growl came from the heart of the jungle, and in another moment a mighty tiger stood before the boy.

"What do you wish, Brother?" the tiger asked.

"O Brother Tiger," said the boy. "The king will kill our mother and make me his slave if, before nightfall, I don't bring him four big, strong tigers to guard the palace gates."

"Wait here for me," the tiger said, and walked back into the forest. The boy waited. Soon the tiger came back, and behind him walked more tigers than the boy could count.

"Get on my back, Brother," the first tiger said. "We will give the king a surprise."

With the boy on his back and the other tigers following, they walked into town. When the people saw them, doors and windows slammed shut.

At the palace the guards wanted to close the gates, but the king ordered them to let the boy and the tigers in.

The court officials paled and trembled as the boy rode up to the throne. He slid off the tiger's back, bowed deeply, and said, "Your Majesty, I have brought you many tigers. Choose any four. They will serve you faithfully."

The king, amazed, chose four of the biggest tigers, sent the rest away, and then allowed the boy to go home.

The boy and his mother were so glad the danger had passed that they did not even think of the reward the king had promised.

But their joy did not last long. The king could not forget the precious jewels, and so he summoned the boy to the palace again.

This time he demanded four peacocks to sit on the corners of the palace roof, or he would kill the mother mouse and make the boy his slave.

Again the boy told his mother what had happened, and again she said, "Do not worry, my son. Your brother the peacock will help us."

She gave the boy the three peacock feathers and told him what to do. When he had thrown the feathers into the air and called, "Brother Peacock," three times, there came the sound of beating wings, and his brother stood beside him.

"What do you wish, Brother?" he asked.

"O Brother Peacock," said the boy. "The king wants four peacocks, to sit on the corners of the palace roof, or he will kill our mother and make me his slave!"

"Wait here, Brother," said the peacock, and soon he

was back with so huge a flock of peacocks behind him that the air grew dark. Four of the big birds grasped the boy in their claws and carried him back to town, and the others followed.

When the townspeople saw the air dense with peacocks, they ran to tell the king, and he seated himself on his throne just as the birds lowered the boy in the palace courtyard. With their tail feathers spread, they grouped themselves around him and marched into the throne room.

"Your Majesty," the boy said, "here are the finest peacocks I could find. Choose any four." The king picked four peacocks, and the rest flew away. Again the boy was allowed to go home with never a word about the promised reward.

Three days passed, and again the king sent for the boy. "I have one last task for you," he said with an evil smile. "This is not a hard one," he chuckled. "I just want your mother to fight our court elephant. If she cannot do this, I shall have her killed and make you my slave."

Again the boy arrived home in tears, but his mother laughed when he told her what the king had demanded.

"This one is easy," she said. "Go and get a long, thin rope and tie it to my tail." The boy did this, put the mouse in his sleeve, and walked to the palace.

There everything was ready for the big event. Banners were flying.

The king sat surrounded by his counselors, and the court elephant, tied by one leg, was standing in a roped-off arena. All the townspeople were gathered to watch.

The boy stood at the edge of the arena, the animal's ties were loosened, and it stepped forward. The mother mouse leaped from the boy's sleeve.

Startled by the sudden movement, the elephant stopped for a moment, and the mouse quickly jumped onto its foot.

Now the elephant wanted to know what was tickling it and put its trunk down. Quickly the little mouse ran up its trunk to its head, down its back, and up and down its legs, all the while winding her rope around the elephant. Back to its head she ran, and round and round, until the animal's big ears were tied flat against its head.

Up and down she ran, so that the elephant was all tangled up, unable to move or even to stand up any longer. He fell down and lay there helplessly.

The spectators cheered and the counselors whispered in the king's ear.

The boy picked up his mother and approached the throne. "Your Majesty," he said, "your three tasks have been carried out. Now give me your daughter and half your kingdom, as you promised."

This time the king had to fulfill his promise, as his counselors advised him. A few years later, when the king died, the boy became king and ruled Nepal, and he brought his mother to live in the palace.